AÌRA

Dedicated to my daughter.

Special thanks to the test readers of this book.

Wilhelm wakes up completely confused in a strange world.

Wilhelm Steiner wakes up in a hospital with no memory of how he got there. He can barely move and lacks the strength to stay conscious. What happened?

In his struggle back to life, Wilhelm uses newly discovered mystical abilities and finds out who did this to him. He wants to leave this part of his semi-legal life behind him, but acquaintances from the past try to prevent that.

Bibliografische Information der Deutschen Nationalbibliothek: Die Deutsche Nationalbibliothek verzeichnet diese Publikation in der Deutschen Nationalbibliografie; detaillierte bibliografische Daten sind im Internet über dnb.dnb.de abrufbar.

Publisher: BoD · Books on Demand GmbH, In de Tarpen 42, 22848 Norderstedt, bod@bod.de
Print: Libri Plureos GmbH, Friedensallee 273, 22763 Hamburg
ISBN: 978-3-7693-1842-5

Cover motif:
Valentin Agapov/Shutterstock.com
Hatteviden/Shutterstock.com
Foxys Forest Manufacture/Shutterstock.com
Ironika/Shutterstock.com

Translation:
The translation of this book from the original german into english was done in the first instance by artificial intelligence (AI) and then corrected by me.
Since I am not a native english speaker, the text may contain errors. Please excuse this.

The author:

Jonathan J. Gugenberger is a passionate philosopher and storyteller who writes down his thoughts in exciting fantasy and science fiction novels.

Visit the author's website:

Table of contents

A personal note:
The translation of this book   10
What has happened so far:
An interesting species   12
What has happened so far:
Finding a human body   20
Chapter 1:
A new life   29
Chapter 2:
Mental powers   56
Chapter 3:
Dismissal   130

A personal note:

The translation of this book

Until that point, readers of my story only had the opportunity to get the german version of the book to read it. Therefore, I had been thinking for some time about having the book translated into other languages, at least into english to start with.

I am not a native englisch Speaker. Admittedly, I am able to speak english to make myself understood in foreign countries – where english is understood – but I knew that this alone is not enough to translate an entire book into this language... I didn't have the money for a professional translation agency, so I put this idea aside. It wasn't realizable at the moment.

But then came artificial intelligence:

After I heard about artificial intelligence and tried some things with it, I noticed that the results that this new technology produced were getting better and better, so after a year I gave the project of „Book translation into english" another chance.

I first asked the artificial intelligence to roughly translate the book. Then I made corrections and other improvements myself.

The result is this book now.

I hope that you, dear readers, enjoy it and forgive any translation errors.

And now the story.

What has happened so far:

An interesting species

Humans! An interesting species!

I hardly knew them back then. Because I had noticed them, I decided at some point to observe them a little more closely. I realised that they lived in some kind of terrarium, which they themselves called earth, and whose ground consisted of liquid and solid rock, covered with fertile soil and water.

The longer I observed the human species, the more interesting they became to me.

I learned a lot about their languages, their cultures and their behaviour.

However, I learnt from a distance, like a pupil who is taught the theory of a subject by a teacher, and soon realised that this was not enough for me. I not only wanted to know how this species behaved, but also why they behaved the way they did. What made humans do what they do?

I thought about what options were available to me to achieve this goal and finally went into direct proximity to Humans in order to study them.

I accompanied them in their daily lives and observed them in their families, professions and intimate moments.

Some of what I saw I could not understand or comprehend, and so I soon realised that it was not enough for me to just observe them. But what else could I do to really understand what drives them?

I thought about it further and came to the conclusion that I had to become a human being myself. I had to feel for myself what cold and warmth feel like. I had to experience for myself what it was like to be hungry, to have joy, to love, to hate.

There were two possibilities.

The first was to create a body for myself to live in as a human being. To be able to do this, however, I first had to analyse one and learn how it works technically.

The second option was to take over a body that was already in life and make it my own.

I weighed up the two options against each other. Each offered many advantages, but also disadvantages.

Creating a new body meant that, without parents, without siblings and without friends, it had no opportunities for social interaction. A large part of human life would therefore remain hidden from me in such a body, so that I would not experience how important these areas of life actually are for humans.

Taking over a living body only worked as long as it was not already inhabited by a spirit - or a soul, as humans call it. However, such a body would have to offer opportunities to experience social life as a human being.

A body cannot live without a spirit. The body belongs to the spirit until it gives it up voluntarily or it is forced to give it up through death.

As a spiritual being, it was therefore not easily possible for me to take a body with belonging ghost – I had to chase the ghost away first. But I didn't want to do that! It was important to me to take over a body that no longer had a spirit living in it. However, such bodies are usually already dead or about to die.

Because I saw it as the only way to really understand human beings, I decided to take over a living body.

But where on earth could I find a human body that was not dead and at the same time no longer inhabited by a spirit?

Moreover, it had to be a body that functioned well enough for me to gain experience with it.

I could only think of one place where there was a possibility of finding such a body: In a hospital.

But it couldn't be just any hospital. It had to be one that had the necessary resources to keep bodies alive that were no longer inhabited by a spirit, but that did not have the ability to bring back the spirit that had originally lived in the body.

I decided that only the hospitals of the rich countries of the twentyfirst century were suitable for this. They were medically advanced enough to keep spiritless bodies alive with machines, but they could not yet bring the spirits back into the restored body, which the hospitals would be able to do in future centuries.

But there were thousands of such hospitals on twentyfirst century on earth, and because I had no other starting points, I decided to use chance ...

As a spiritual being, I only need to mentally go to a place in order to travel there.

So I imagined myself in a hospital in a rich country of the twentyfirst century. Because I left it open which hospital it exactly should be, chance intervened here.

In my imagination, I was in the coma ward of one of these hospitals. In comatose patients, the ghost is often no longer in possession of the body, so I had a good chance of finding a body for myself here.

A moment later, as usual when travelling to an unknown destination, something began to pull on me. Stronger and stronger, as if I was hanging on to a rope that someone was pulling with great force. The pulling force set me in motion and I was propelled towards my destination with ever-increasing speed.

I travelled over forests and rivers, over towns and wasteland, over apartment blocks and skyscrapers until I reached my destination.

The travelling speed slowed as I neared my destination, becoming slower and slower until I finally slid through the walls on the first floor of a hospital and came to a standstill in a hospital room.

What has happened so far:

Finding a human body

There was only one patient in this room, which amazed me. From my observations, I knew that people in this era were normally hospitalised in multi-bed rooms. Only a few had the funds to afford a private room in a hospital.

The patient was lying in the sickbed and, with the exception of his arms and head, was covered by a duvet. His arms, wrapped in partly bloody bandages, lay loosely on the blanket. His head, except for his nose and mouth, was almost completely wrapped in bandages, which were also bloody. Two thin tubes led from his nose, each from a nostril, to a medical device. His chest rose and fell. Tubes were also attached to both arms, and wires led from under the blanket to other medical devices. One of them beeped at regular intervals.

Two questions now arose: How serious were his injuries? And was the patient's body still inhabited by a spirit?

If the injuries were too big, I would need too much time to heal them. In principle, this was not a big problem, but the further the healing of the body progressed, the greater the risk that another spirit being would take advantage of my healing success and claim the body before me. I wanted to prevent that. The healing should therefore be completed as quickly as possible.

The more important of the two questions, whether the body was still inhabited by a spirit being, could be answered by my following procedure:

I laid myself over the body like a blanket and tried to feel it, like a blind person trying to feel the surface of an object.

This was the first step in taking over a body. If it was still inhabited by a spirit being, I would be able to perceive that during this process.

The second step was to increase the feeling to such an extent that the body merged with myself.

However, this normally only happens if the body is not too severely injured.

So I tried to feel the body and thus clarify the question of whether a spirit being was still connected to the body ...

When I realised that there was no longer a spirit being in this body, I analysed the injuries.

Because I had no idea how the human body is constructed - this was my first journey into such a body - my approach was to compare every single cell with all the other cells. I took the state that most of the cells were in as the desired state and assumed that all cells that deviated from this were at least defective or even destroyed. In this way I came to the following diagnosis:

The body had numerous broken bones, especially the ribs were affected. Some of the internal organs of the upper body were severely bruised, others were slightly bruised. The skin showed abrasions and blood stains. I also recognised a contusion of the brain.

Were there too many injuries? That would become clear during the healing process I was about to begin.

Again, I took the condition of the cells that I had identified as undamaged as a basis and modified the remaining cells so that they functioned like the basic cells. I did this by repairing the parts of the cells that I had identified as defective with new cell material. I couldn't reuse existing but damaged material or break it down into its atoms to get rid of it, so I built around these parts so that they could subsequently be disassabled by the body's own repair system, which hopefully still worked. However, this slowed down the healing process considerably.

In this way, I gradually restored the body to what I assumed was a healthy state. However, I could only repair the cells themselves. If they had contained any kind of information before they were damaged, it would have been that these were lost now. This was particularly true of the cells in the brain. These could have stored thoughts, feelings, experiences and information about how the body works and how to move it.

I healed the injuries that were obvious to me, such as broken bones and skin abrasions, first, then those that were less clearly recognisable as injuries. With some cells, I needed several attempts before they worked again. But there were also cells where my healing was unsuccessful. This prolonged the healing process once again.

Nurses came into the room from time to time and took care to the body. Doctors rolled him out along with the bed and brought him back into the room later, or they checked the body's functions right there in the room. The more the healing progressed, the more they whispered to each other in the presence of the body and looked at the test results in amazement. During the daily bandage changes, they realised that the abrasions and bruises were either already healed or the healing was well advanced. The bandages were removed at some point and the remaining injuries were covered with large plasters. Visitors kept coming into the room. Sometimes they were men in groups of two or three, sometimes they came individually. Women also came by, in groups or individually. The visitors grabbed a chair and sat next to the bed. Some read aloud from a book, others talked to the body or listened to music with it.

At some point I decided that the body had healed sufficiently to take it over. The healing would continue with the body's own resources anyway. So I started the takeover.

I tried to feel the body even more than I already did, my hands, arms, feet, legs, neck, upper body, head and face, one after the other, as if they were my own body parts.

Images, knowledge, feelings and sounds suddenly appeared out of nowhere. These came from the brain. So there were definitely still brain cells that had stored information that I could retrieve. They came in no particular order and were completely jumbled up without forming a context.

Unfortunately, this storm of thoughts was over to quickly for me to understand any of it.

Slowly, I began to perceive the individual body parts as my own. I docked more and more onto the body until the takeover was complete and the body had become mine.

Chapter 1:

A new life

I open my eyes. It is bright. Very bright! My eyes hurt. The pain forces me to close them. I try to open them again. Again it is very bright and again the pain forces me to close them. But this time I manage to keep them open a little longer. The pain eases a little this second time. So I try again and again and at some point, I manage to keep my eyes open. But a slight pain remains.

I look round. The image is blurred. Where am I? In a room. I squint my eyes tightly and open them again. Everything is still blurry. I feel strange. Like I've been asleep for years. I try to move my arms. That hurts too. My arms feel heavy. So I leave it.

What's going on here? I have the feeling that something is completely wrong. Something is completely different than it should be!

I am tired, very tired. I close my eyes. Just for a few minutes ...

„Mr Steiner? Can you hear me?"

What is that? Who is that calling? Who is Mr Steiner?

„Please open your eyes if you can hear me, Mr Steiner."

Someone touches me and I open my eyes. They still hurt a little, but not as much as before. I pinch my eyelids together a little, which reduces the pain.

„Nice to have you back", says a tall, slim man in a white coat, looking at me.

I can see the man clearly, my bed too. The rest of the room remains blurred.

He talks to me in a loud voice and has a big grin on his face.

„Mr Steiner, do you understand me?"

I assume that I am Mr Steiner, so I nod.

„Look at my finger, please."

He holds his hand in front of my eyes, his fingers are slightly formed into a fist and his index finger is outstretched. I look at this finger. He shines with something into both of my eyes, first the left, then the right. When the bright light hits my eyes, the pain intensifies again. I close them again.

„Mr Steiner, I'm Doctor Koller", he finally introduces himself. „You're in a hospital. Do you know what that means?"

A hospital? Something has obviously happened to me.

„Why am I here?", I ask.

My words come slurring out of my mouth, some sounds get stuck in them. I can't fully hear what I'm saying myself. But Doctor Koller seems to understand me.

„You were injured."

A pitiful, barely comprehensible:

„Aha", comes out of my mouth.

„Get some more sleep. I'll come back to see you later. Then we'll sort everything out", says the doctor and leaves the room.

I'm still very tired and my eyes still hurt. So I close them and give them some rest.

When I regain consciousness, my eyes open of their own accord. The pain has disappeared. I still feel tired, but much more energised than before. Unfortunately, my vision of the room is still blurred.

Something is dangling directly in front of my face and I can see it clearly. It's round, flat and there's a coloured bulge in the middle.

There are symbols on the bulge that look familiar to me.

What are these symbols? Do they have a meaning? I take a closer look at them, symbol by symbol.

Little by little, it's as buried knowledge is resurfacing as the symbols slowly make sense. I recognise a N, an U, an R, an S, and a E. The word nurse forms in my head and I even know what a nurse is.

Why is this thing dangling here? Can I do something with it?

I try to collect myself first and analyse the situation.

What has happened? Why am I here? And... what kind of room is this? I remember that not so long ago there was a man in the room who told me that I had been injured.

Some doctor, if I remember correctly.

So I was injured. The doctor said I was in hospital.

So that's two questions answered. Maybe the nurse knows something about what happened to me. I could try calling ... But how?

The dangling thing is still hanging in front of my face - maybe I can call him with it? I pick it up, realising that my arm and hand movements are sluggish and imprecise.

I feel the bulge that has the text „nurse" on it with my thumb and examine the whole thing more closely. I unintentionally press a little on the bulge. After a few seconds, while I'm still examining it, there's a knock on the door and someone comes in.

I can't recognise anything apart from a blurred outline. The outline comes closer, slowly becomes sharper and turns more and more into a man who, as he stands by my bed, is clearly visible.

He is quite muscular, tall, but slightly smaller than the doctor.

As he stands by my bed, I let go of the dangling thing.

„Hello, Mr Steiner", he greets me.

„What can I do for you?"

„Hello", I reply. „I was wondering if you knew anything about what exactly happened to me. I know that I was injured. But how exactly did that happen?"

„I'm afraid I don't know", he replies.

With a wave of his hand, he looks at an object at the lower end of his arm and says:

„But the doctor should be coming to check on you soon. You can ask him then. He should be with you in about fifteen to thirty minutes."

„Okay. All right, thanks", I say, a little disappointed. The male nurse nods curtly and leaves the room.

So waiting for fifteen to thirty minutes ...

Then I'll rest for a while until the doctor arrives, I think. I close my eyes and relax.

The door opens and someone comes in. As with the male nurse earlier, I can only make out a blurred outline, which becomes clearer as I get closer.

When he arrives at my bedside, he introduces himself, now clearly visible, as Doctor Koller.

„How are you doing?", he asks me.

„Really good, but I'm quite confused. I'd like to know what happened. How exactly did I hurt?"

„Well, according to the police, you were beaten up. We don't know more details at the moment. But the police want to ask you a few questions in due course anyway. Maybe you'll find out more details then", he replies.

„But, Mr Steiner, I also have to ask you a few more questions in order to check that everything is all right with you. Is it convenient for you right now, or should I come back later?"

I don't really care about what he wants to ask, I just want to know what has happened to me. That's why I answer in frustration:

„I don't care."

„Then I'll ask you the most important questions now, the others will follow later on", he decides. „If you have problems answering one or more of the questions, there's no need to worry. Sometimes it takes a little time for all the memories to come back."

I nod slightly, signalling that I have understood, whereupon the doctor begins to ask his questions:

„What's your first name?"

Still frustrated, I open my mouth and take a breath to answer his seemingly ridiculously simple question.

But as I move, I realise that I don't know the answer! I have no idea what my first name is. Even after thinking about it for a few seconds, I still owe him my answer.

„I don't know ...", is therefore my answer.

What's wrong with me? Why don't I know that? While I'm completely surprised and a little panic slowly rises inside me, the doctor moves on to the next question.

„When were you born?"

Another question that seems as if it couldn't be easier. I open my mouth again, this time a little more cautiously and thoughtfully. Do I know the answer now?

No! I don't know again! The whole situation makes me desperate. My eyes fill with tears. Completely despondent, with a slightly tearful voice, I ask:

„What's wrong with me?"

The doctor obviously deduces from my reaction that I don't know the answer and that I am panicking.

„Mr Steiner, calm down. It's not so bad that you don't remember some things. You have laid in a coma for a long time. That and the mishandling were a great strain on your body. It first has to recover from this.

Don't worry about it. Your injuries have healed fairly quickly over the last few weeks. If your body continues to recover so great, your memories will return soon."

He takes a short break.

„Get some rest. That can also help you remember some things."

He says goodbye with the words

„We'll leave the questions for now. We'll have plenty of time for that in the next few days", and leaves the room.

When he's gone, I think. What do I know about myself at all? What do I know about my life?

I realise that I don't know anything. Neither where I live, nor how old I am. Do I have a family? Who are my parents? It feels like I've just been born. Everything is so strange!

My body! The world! Simply everything!

But the doctor said that it would get better. And if he says that, hopefully it will be true.

I try to relax and calm down, but I don't succeed very well. At some point, I am calm enough to feel reasonably relaxed.

After a while, I alternate between phases of deep relaxation, in which I sink into myself, and phases in which I am fully awake but relaxed. I have the feeling that the phases of immersion do me a lot of good and energise me.

I'm in a phase of good relaxation, letting thoughts come and go, when there's a knock on the door. A moment later, it opens and someone enters the room.

As before, I can't see this person clearly, but I recognise immediately that it can't be the doctor or the male nurse. The indistinct outline doesn't match to either of them.

On approaching, he turns out to be an attractive young woman. She has long, curly, reddish hair that falls to her shoulders and an incredibly pretty face. Her whole figure looks familiar, as if I've seen her before.

When she arrives at my bedside, she gives me a kiss on the cheek.

„Hello, my darling! I'm so happy that you're feeling better again!" she says in a voice that is both joyful and worried at the same time. „Do you remember who I am?"

This woman calls me „My darling", I wonder.

So far I have always been addressed as Mr Steiner. Does she know me better?

„You look familiar to me. As if I've seen you before. How is your name?", I say.

When she calls me „My darling", I decide to call her by her first name. Equal rights for all.

„Oh, man, they really did a number on you", she says.

She smiles at me. A sympathetic but forced smile.

Every now and then, her smile seems to slip away and become something else. Does she want to cry?

She takes my hand in hers.

„But don't worry. I'm convinced that everything will be fine. We'll take advantage of every possible therapy that can help you in some way. It will be fine."

Her smile slips again and her face briefly contorts into tears. A few moments later, she finds her smile again and says:

„Then let me introduce myself. I'm your girlfriend Barbara! How are you?"

Her question triggers the feeling of despair in me again, so that my eyes fill with tears. I don't want to feel this feeling, so I swallow it and answer:

„Well, that's about it ... It all feels so strange. I can't not remember.

I've forgotten everything! And there's something wrong with my eyes, I see everything so blurred."

Barbara's eyes are moist again as well.

„I know, my darling! The hospital rang me when you woke up and explained everything to me. I was told that everything could be okay and you simply need time to recover. So don't worry about it. Just ask me what you want to know. Then we can work together to get you back to your old self."

Still with tears in my eyes, I ask her a series of questions that seem most important to me at the moment, and Barbara answers each one with a smile on her face. I keep interrupting her explanations because I don't understand some of the words. She patiently explains everything I want to know until I understand everything.

Her explanations help me forget my despair for a while, and Barbara also seems to feel better little by little.

In between, she opens one of the lower drawers on a box to the right of my bed and takes out an object.

„Here, your glasses. They'll help you see everything clearly again", she says and hands them to me.

I look at the glasses in surprise and don't really know what to do with them.

„Glasses? ... What do I do with it?"

She takes it out of my hand and puts it on my nose.

„Better?"

I am amazed by the suddenly sharp image that reveals to me and say: „Ahaa!".

I found out from Barbara that my name is Wilhelm Steiner. I'm thirty-five years old and live with my girlfriend, Barbara Schacher, who is thirty-four years old, in a cosy house on the outskirts of the city.

I have been working quite successfully as a lawyer in a large law company for five years.

Barbara is a chemist and works for a small company in the outskirts.

According to her, we met for the first time at a ski lift while waiting for a free gondola.

We boarded this gondola together with our friends and had a great talk during the journey. When we then had lunch in the same restaurant and talked again very well, we exchanged telephone numbers as we said goodbye.

Later, we arranged to go to the cinema.

Unfortunately, there wasn't a film showing that we were interested in. So we didn't go to the cinema that evening, but simply went for a walk. We walked around for a very long time and talked and laughed together.

We repeated these walks a few times until we decided to sit down in front of the TV at her home, completely casually. That evening we became a couple!

Eight weeks ago, I was beaten up by some insane people. I've been in hospital ever since.

After all! Now my past is no longer completely in the dark.

After she has told me everything, she stays with me for a while.

„Just so you're not so lonely", she explains.

Their presence actually makes me feel better and less lost.

Just before she leaves, she asks me if I need anything before she gives me a kiss on the cheek and promises to come back soon.

I have become very tired in the meantime. Barbara's stories keep me busy. I would love to be able to remember that time. She recounted our meeting with such a sparkle in her eyes, and I want to feel that sparkle too!

As I think about her and myself and how nice it would be to be able to remember again, I get more and more tired. I put my glasses on the nightstand Barbara took them out of earlier, close my eyes and relax.

When I open my eyes again, I feel very well rested and for a few seconds, I am filled with peace. Then I feel the anxiety of the previous day again.

I remember experiencing something between closing my eyes yesterday and opening them today. I was trapped in something. What I was trapped in kept me small and insignificant. I was incapable of doing anything. It was like being in a prison from which I could not escape. A prison of thoughts maybe.

That was strange. Because I can't remember any similar incidents from my past, I conclude that there is obviously another world besides this world, my girlfriend, the room, the hospital where I'm lying in bed trying to get better. I find that very interesting! I should talk to Barbara about it. Maybe she can explain it to me.

I want to get up and walk around a bit. So I grab the duvet to put it aside when something pinches the pit of my arm.

When I look, I realise that a tube is stuck in it. I check the other arm and notice a tube there too.

Damn! If I want to get up, someone has to take these tubes off me first. Can the male nurse do that? I call him by pressing the red button on the remote control.

After a few minutes, someone opens the door and looks into the room. I put on my glasses, see that it's the nurse and tell him what I want.

„Unfortunately, I can't do that. Only a doctor is allowed to do that", he replies to my request.

„I'll let Doctor Koller know. He'll take care of you then", he promises me.

„Do you have any idea when the doctor will be free?", I ask him.

„I don't know, but it will probably be around midday or shortly before. He has a lot to do today."

Without waiting for an answer from me, he disappears and the door is closed.

So, waiting for the doctor. Again ...

I try to relax for as long as I can, but the longer I wait for the doctor, the more restless I become. It feels like doing nothing is slowly eating me up.

Maybe the nurse knows what to do in a situation like this, I think to myself, so I call him again. Soon he opens the door again and asks:

„Yes, do you need anything else?"

„Listen, it's going to be a long time before the doctor comes to see me. What can I do in the meantime?"

He thinks for a moment.

„Just a moment, I'll bring you something to read." With that, he disappears again. A few minutes later, he returns with a pile of something. I can't see exactly what he's holding, but I assume it's the magazines he's announced.

He puts them down with the words:

„Here you go, maybe there`s something useful for you", on the nightstand next to my bed.

I thank him. When he has left the room, I take a small pile of them to my bed.

Again, my arms and hands feel sluggish and their movements imprecise. But it's enough to browse through the magazines for a while.

Some pages are full of pictures, on others there is only or almost only text. And it is precisely this text that interests me. I want to recognise its meaning. Perhaps it will bring back buried knowledge and memories.

I can't decipher it at the moment, but the characters look familiar to me, just like the word „Nurse" on the dangling thing above my bed. So I take a closer look. Again, symbol by symbol. And indeed! Little by little, buried knowledge comes to light again. In this way, I recognise many words and numbers in the magazines and remember their meaning.

That takes a while ...

At some point, there's a knock on the door and the doctor comes in. He stands in front of my bed and greets me:

„Hello, Mr Steiner. I hear you'd like to get up and walk around a bit. That makes

49

me happy! That's a very good sign. I've also heard that you've already been given something to read."

He looks with pleasure at the pile of magazines in the bed and on the nightstand next to the bed.

„Have you managed to read anything in it yet?", he asks me.

„Yes, I have. It takes a little time at first with new letters and words, but after some thinking about it I am able to understand them again", I report proudly.

„That's very good! Then I'll have a look at your vital signs. Maybe I can disconnect you from the devices."

He looks at a monitor next to my bed and nods slightly. Then he moves to another device next to the monitor and presses a button, whereupon it buzzes softly for a moment and outputs a piece of paper. The doctor takes it and looks at it for a few seconds.

He nods contentedly and says:

„Your values are completely normal again, Mr Steiner. So I'll remove the connections now."

He switches off the devices from which he has just read the values and then carefully removes the tubes from my arms.

Then he asks me to move my arms slightly to a side so that he can push my nightdress top up. He now also removes some of the connections from my upper body that I hadn't even noticed before.

„I'll have a quick look at the rest of the wounds too", he finally says and checks all the plasters that are still stuck to my body one by one.

„You have extremely good wound healing!", he says at some point in between.

When all the plasters have been removed, he explains:

„So, now for some organisational matters.

Mr Steiner. As it is no longer necessary to feed you artificially, you will have to eat solid food again from today evening on. Some meal will be put together for you until evening. You will receive a menu plan for the rest of the week tomorrow morning. Please fill it out and give it to the nurse."

I don't know what a menu plan is, but I assume that I will realise it when I see it.

„Then I have a schedule for you here. It lists all the therapies for this week and next week. These should help you to recover even faster. The nurse will pick you up and take you to the therapy rooms", he continues, placing the schedule on top of the remaining pile of magazines on my nightstand.

„One more thing: before you stand up for the first time, please ask the therapist if he agrees. He is the best person to judge whether you have enough strength to do this. If you are given permission, please let the nurse know. He will support you while you walk."

Just before he leaves the room, he asks:

„Do you have any further questions that I can answer?"

I shake my head.

„No, thank you. Everything is clear so far."

Then the doctor leaves the room.

Because I'm not allowed to get up yet - unfortunately I have to wait again. This time for the therapist - I look at the therapy plan. Again, there are lots of unknown signs and words on it.

I use the same tactic as with the magazines and the „Nurse" lettering and soon recognise the meaning. I also notice that the time between taking a closer look and recognising the meaning of signs and words is getting shorter.

According to the plan, I have two therapies a day, each of which lasts about an hour.

The first one is planned for this afternoon at two pm, it's a physiotherapy session.

Well, I'm looking forward to that. Then I can ask the therapist straight away if I can get up.

But how do I know when it's time for the therapy? The doctor has said that the nurse will pick me up, but I want to be able to prepare myself mentally for the therapy beforehand.

I take a closer look around the room. Maybe I'll find something I can use to tell the time.

There is an indefinable device on the nightstand next to my bed. It has numbers from zero to nine on it. I analyse the device and pick it up. Something connected to the device falls off as if it were part of it. It emits a rapidly repeating sound that sounds known. I have also seen a device like this before.

How do I know these two things?

I think about it and recognise the device, coupled with the sound, as a telephone. The thing that is attached to the device is the telephone receiver. I carefully place it back on its recess and put both back on the nightstand.

I let my eyes wander further.

There is a machine hanging on the wall in the right-hand corner as seen from my bed. I've also seen this before. I take a closer look at it, but don't recognise all its details because it's hanging too far away, so I can't make sense of it.

So I continue to look around. On the wall to my left is a round disc with numbers from one to twelve on it.

Using the same tactics as with the telephone, I recognise the disc as a clock.

The small clock-hand points to twelve, the big one to ten, so it's now ten minutes before twelve o'clock.

That means I have less than two hours until my first therapy session.

Because I am not allowed to get up yet I decide to get some more rest.

Chapter 2:

Mental powers

„Mr Steiner?"

I am rudely torn from my rest.

The nurse stands next to my bed and has a wheelchair next to him.

For the first time, I notice that the clothes of the doctors I've dealt with so far are similar to those of the nurses. Both are dressed in white. White shirt, white trousers, white socks and white shoes. Only a sign attached to the shirt at chest height reads „Nurse".

„Therapy is about to start and you still need to change your clothes."

„Change clothes?" I repeat, confused and a little sleepy.

„Yes, you can't come to training in your pyjamas," replies the nurse.

He opens one of the wardrobes to the right of the bed and takes out two neatly folded items of clothing. He places them on the foot of the bed and then helps me out of my pyjamas and into my clothes. Only now do I realise how weak my legs are. I can hardly move them.

With the words

„All right, now please get into the wheelchair", he skilfully lifts me from the bed

58

into the wheelchair and takes me out of the room into a long corridor.

I notice arrows and lines on the floor of the corridor and on the walls. Curtain places in a hospital are written on the lines. When I ask the nurse what they mean, he explains that they are signposts. In this way, the management tries to prevent anyone from getting lost.

It turns out that the patients rooms are on the first floor and the therapy rooms are on the second floor, so we take the lift up one floor.

It is a relatively large room with all kinds of therapeutic equipment on the walls. There is a mat on the floor near one wall. Next to it is a treadmill with handrails on both sides and a hanging device over it. There are three doors at the rear of the room.

A man stands waiting in front of the mat. Like the doctors and nurses, he is dressed completely in white.

The nurse drives me to him.

„Hello, Mr Steiner! We will work together to ensure that you are able to walk normally again soon", the man greets me and shakes my hand. „I've heard that you're already making huge progress. That makes me very happy. You were in a coma for eight weeks. That doesn't leave your joints, bones and muscles unaffected."

He starts the therapy.

„All right, then. Let's take a few steps together. I'd like to see how you're using your legs at the moment."

My first thought is that I'm about to find out how well I can get out of the wheelchair on my own, but the nurse is already there to help me by hooking me in and lifting my upper body. Once I have a good foothold, the therapist asks me:

„Please try to move your legs so that they go forwards. You don't need to be afraid of falling over, we'll support you."

Now the therapist is also getting involved and giving me additional support.

I try to move my right leg forwards and put my foot on the floor. The leg moves, but only hesitantly and imprecisely. Because I am convinced that I can do better, I put more force into the movement. As a result, the leg bounces further forwards than I intended.

„Very good! That's very good!", is the therapist's reaction.

„Now shift your weight from one leg to the other."

So I shift my weight, which works perfectly.

„Now please try to put your free leg forwards."

With these words, he taps me with his hand on the leg on which there is no weight.

I move it forwards. This leg also bounces forwards more than I want it to. And the therapist praises me here too. I realise that tapping my leg with one hand helps me a lot to decide which leg to move.

We walk around the room a few times in this way. I know quite quickly which leg needs to be moved and when, even without the therapist tapping on the respective leg. But he keeps doing it. What I lack is the strength in my legs. As a result, they keep making this bouncing movement.

Until the end of the lesson, we practise sitting down, standing up, walking a few lengths, sitting down again and doing it all over again. In between, the nurse gives me a water bottle every now and then so that I can drink something.

It's all very exhausting and draining. So I'm glad when it's over and I can sit back in my wheelchair and lean back.

Finally, the therapist says:

„That was a very successful hour. You can be very pleased with yourself. We have achieved a lot."

With a very tired „thank you", I say goodbye to him and decide not to ask him if I can walk on my own. The lesson has obviously shown that walking without help is not possible at the moment.

When I get back to my room, I am lifted into bed, put my glasses back on the nightstand and sink completely into sleepiness.

When the nurse wakes me up, dinner has already been served. He takes me to a table at the foot of my bed and sits me down on a chair. I'm far too tired to eat and drift off into sleepiness with every bite.

At some point, the nurse picks me up and takes me back to bed. As soon as I'm lying down, I let the tiredness carry me away.

After a while, I suddenly feel a foreign hand wrapping my own. I look up, very tired. I can barely open my eyes. I can see Barbara's face very blurred. She is holding my hand in hers.

When she realises that I'm awake, she gives me her best smile! Her eyes become moist. She whispers barely audibly:

„I love you!"

„Me too", I whisper with all the strength I still have. I am actually very happy about her presence and her love.

It's strange, on the one hand I have no conscious memory of our life together, on the other hand I feel so comfortable and attracted to her when she's with me. With this feeling, I close my eyes again and let myself drift away without resistance.

When I open my eyes the next morning, I feel like I could tear out trees. There is an incredibly cosy, warm feeling in my stomach and I could hug everyone.

As I move a litte in bed, I realise that the muscles in my legs and arms are aching.

I'm also hungry. It's the first time I feel it, but I know what it means. The doctor said something about getting a menu plan today. I still don't know what it is, but from what the doctor said yesterday, I think it might have something to do with food.

I hardly have finished my thought as the door opens. I put on my glasses and see a stocky, muscular-looking woman in white clothing, shorter than the male nurse or one of the doctors, with short-cropped hair. As she approach, I see from her sign that she is one of the nurses.

„Good morning, Mr Steiner!", she announces happily. „Did you sleep well?"

„I slept very well", I reply in a good mood.

„Very good! I hope you're hungry."

I smile broadly and look forward to the food. She puts a tray on the table.

„This is your breakfast. Would you like to eat in bed or at the table?"

„At the table, please", I decide.

„All right", she says, „but before breakfast you should brush your teeth, take a shower and put everyday cloths on. Do you need help with that?"

I'm not quite sure what she means by brushing her teeth and showering, but my feeling says that it's important. That's why I want her to show me these things.

„Yes", I answer her.

„All right! Hang on, I'll be right back", she says, leaves the room and returns shortly afterwards with a wheelchair, which she skilfully lifts me into. She then puts me into the bathroom and helps me brush my teeth and take a shower.

In the bathroom, she shows me everything I need to know about washing my body in the morning and evening, brushing my teeth and shaving my face from time to time.

The bathroom is very well equipped for people who have problems with their muscles. There are fold-out seats opposite the washbasin and in the shower, and there are grab rails all over the walls.

After my morning hygiene, she puts me back again and lifts me onto the bed. She takes new clothes and helps me put them on.

I realise, especially when I'm changing, that I now have more feeling in my legs than yesterday during training. When I finished clothing, she helps me to the table so that I can eat there.

„This is the menu plan, by the way", she points with her index finger to a piece of paper on the tray, which is wedged between two plates.

„When you've finished your breakfast, please mark the meals you'd like to eat this week. If you need help eating, just press here", she continues, pointing to a button on the wall directly above the table labelled „Nurse".

„Otherwise, I wish you a blessed meal!" With that, she leaves the room.

I look at the tray. What is there?

There are two pieces of pastry in a basket.

Next to them on a small plate are jars, one with butter, one with jam and one with a chocolate spread. In front of each jar is a small piece of paper with the contents written on it. A jug of Tea and a small plate with a knife on it are placed next to it. I enjoy everything and look at the menu plan. Apparently today is Thursday. Monday, Tuesday and Wednesday are crossed out. A note has been added to Thursday. It reads: „Today", and a small arrow has been added for Thursday.

There is a choice of two soups every day:

pancake soup and noodle soup.

I can also choose a main course each day. These are different every day. Because I don't know exactly what I'm going to get for many dishes and how it taste anyway, I let chance decide.

The first thing I want to try today is noodle soup. I have a good feeling about that.

Tomorrow I will also have noodle soup and the two remaining days after that I will have pancake soup. So far, so good.

Now I'd like to go back to bed and read the rest of the magazines I didn't get round to yesterday. This improves my reading and brings back knowledge that I thought was lost.

I also have to look at which therapies I have today and when they take place.

Because the doctor has forbidden me to stand up without help for the moment, I press the „Nurse" button on the wall, wait until the nurse arrives and let her help me back into bed. The first thing I do there is check when the next therapy session starts. At 10:15 am. This time it's meditation.

It's now seven o'clock. That means I have plenty of time to read the magazines and get some rest in between.

As I keep turning the pages of the magazine and lifting them up so that I can read them at eye level, I notice that the more I work with my arms and hands, the easier it is to control them. However, they also hurt more.

At around ten o'clock, the nurse comes to pick me up for therapy. She puts me into the wheelchair she has brought with her and takes me to the second floor.

The therapy room is slightly smaller than the room I was in yesterday, but is very cosily furnished. I notice a pleasant smell and feel very comfortable straight away. All I really need to relax completely in here is a bed.

The therapist comes to me and greets me with a handshake.

„Hello, Mr Steiner! Please come in. Please, sit on this chair here", he points with his right-hand to one of two chairs facing each other. The nurse lifts me up and takes me to the chair. Of course I help as much as I can. I want my legs to regain their strength as quickly as possible.

As I sit in the chair, the therapist asks me:

„Have you ever meditated before?"

I shake my head.

„No. Not that I know of."

„Okay, no problem", he says. „I'll explain the basics to you now and then we'll try it together."

I nod.

He explains to me for a few minutes what the point of meditating is and what it could do for me in my situation if I do it properly.

He then asks me to implement his instructions as far as I am able.

„Mr Steiner", he begins the therapy,

„Please concentrate on your breath. Be aware of how you breathe in and how you breathe out, how your chest rises and falls."

The therapist breathes audibly together with me.

„Breathe in."

The therapist and me breathe in.

„Do you notice how your chest rises?"

I feel my chest raise and want to respond, but I have the feeling that he doesn't expect an answer. So I say nothing and continue to listen to his words.

„And ... you breathe out again."

We exhale together.

„Do you notice how your chest sinks?"

I notice how my chest sinks. Because I already know that the therapist doesn't expect an answer, I don't say anything in response to this question either. After three or four repetitions, he stops commenting and it becomes quiet in the room, except for the sound of our breathing. We continue to breathe together in this way for some time until at some point he says in a very quiet tone of voice:

„Now imagine that your body and mind are completely healed. Rejoice in the fact that your body and mind have recovered so quickly and that you will soon be back to your old self. Let the feeling of joy grow and grow."

I try to visualise the things accordingly and use memories from yesterday's therapy, when the therapist praised me and I was happy about it. I also use the doctor's praise for my healing success so far to actually feel the joy.

At first I only manage a little, but then more and more. Shortly before the therapist initiates the next phase, I can feel the joy of my success without having to imagine the praise from the doctor and the therapist.

The therapist leads me through a few more exercises in which I am always asked to visualise something different. Sometimes it's how I go for a completely healthy walk and how I am really happy about my healthy body, or how my muscles grow to make them strong again as quickly as possible.

After a while, he brings me back to the here and now:

„Now become aware of the smells and sounds in this room again. Become aware of where you are. Feel your body ... your arms ... your legs ... feel your face ..."

Again I try to follow his instructions.

After we have finished the meditation, he asks me how I enjoyed the lesson and what problems I had during it.

I answer his questions, whereupon he thanks me and, after calling the nurse, he says goodbye to me.

A few minutes later, the nurse opens the door. She lifts me into the wheelchair again and takes me back to my room. Once there, she helps me into bed and leaves the room.

The clock reads 11:25.

It was good for me to meditate, but I still feel tired and decide to rest a little until lunch.

For lunch, we have chicken-legs with rice and vegetables as well as the noodle soup we ordered. At least that's what it says on the notes leaning against the plates. The nurse has put the food on a tray on the table, as she did in the morning, lifted me off the bed, sat me in an chair by the table and then left the room with the words „If you need anything else, just call."

The next training starts at 3:00 pm. According to the training plan today arm and finger exercises are next. I still have almost three hours until then.

I'm a bit frustrated that I constantly have to call the nurse when I want to go somewhere. Now I'd like to find a quiet room to meditate for a while. I want to forget this world with its nurses, the times when there is nothing to do and a certain powerlessness, at least for a short time, and concentrate fully on meditation.

Once again, I call the nurse and ask her if she can take me to the meditation room. She fetches a wheelchair and takes me to a large room on the second floor. The equipment in this room is the same as in the room where I had the meditation session with the trainer this morning. I let the nurse take me to a free seat and start to put what I have learnt into practice.

After a few minutes, I'm very calm, but unlike when I'm meditating with the trainer, my thoughts keep coming to the fore.

I look at it briefly and then push it away from me ...

After a while, these thoughts become less and less prominent and eventually disappear completely. A cosy, warm and constantly calm feeling sets in that I can't remember ever having felt before.

I enjoy this wonderful feeling, and after a while it feels as if the world around me can't harm me anymore. As if I were the one, that decides about what happens to me and what not. Some time later it seems as if my body is beginning to disintegrate. As if it was becoming less and less relevant to my life.

With progressing of the meditation all these sensations become stronger and stronger. Until I enter a new state of being. My body is still there, but not much more than a cover that you can put on and take off as you want. I am just a ghost myself.

Did the meditation teacher mean this state when he spoke of trance? Probably.

Although my body has closed its eyes, I can see everything around me. I particularly notice my body, which is still meditating. It is breathing slowly and calmly.

The meditation room now has a completely different effect on me. As if I no longer belong in this world. As if this world was just something I was observing. I feel like I'm finally back home, finally free again.

Everything will be fine now!

Suddenly I remember things that I recognise as my past, and I sense that these memories do not belong to my body. I want to know what's behind them and try to awake them ...

I remember that I was researching something in the past. For the purpose of this research, I wanted to get very close to it.

I also remember that I analysed my body. But for what purpose? I sense that the knowledge is there. Again I think hard ...

Little by little I remember that I explored humanity and that this was done from a distance. I remember that it was too theoretical and I wanted to experience for myself what it was like to be human... Did I then perhaps try to live as a human?

And how do these memories fit in with the attack on my body and the coma? Is there any connection at all?

The doctor said, when he removed the bandages and connections, that my body was healing unusually quickly... What if this rapid healing had something to do with an attempt to become human? Did I possibly heal a comatose body and then make it my own?

At least that would explain a lot.

If these assumptions are correct, I should now be able to heal my brain enough to gain access to his memories. I decide to give it a try and set my mind to the task of the attention to the cells of the brain.

As if I had done this before, I analyse the cells as a matter of course and very quickly I come to the conclusion that there is nothing to repair. As far as I can see, all the cells are functioning as they should. But then why can't I access the memories? Do they need some kind of stimulus, and if so, what kind?

As if I already knew the answer, I suddenly get a feeling that I would spontaneously describe as intuition, although I didn't know what it was until just now. According to this feeling, I have to concentrate on the cells and communicate with them. I have to ask them to transfer the information, that means the memories, to me.

I decide to try it out right away and once again focus my attention on the cells. I try to send the request that their memories be transferred to me.

Nothing happens at first. Then I realise that information is suddenly being transmitted. I see images, hear sounds, receive knowledge and feel emotions.

Slowly at first, then faster and faster. All of a sudden, all kinds of information come crashing in on me. The information comes so quickly and completely without context that I am unable to absorb it, even more not to understand them ...

So I ask the cells to send the information again, but this time I ask them to do it more slowly.

After a few seconds, the information comes back, just as incoherent, but much slower. As a result, I am now able to take in the wealth of information and understand some of it. However, some memories are still too jumbled to recognise any context. But the good thing is that I know now a lot more about my body and the world it lives in.

Unfortunately, I received very little information about how my body was beaten up and became hospitalised. I only felt the fear that the body had and how painful the wounds were.

There is also some information missing about Barbara. For example, I only have fragmentary information about how we got to know each other. Some of these memories are linked to feelings, others are images or sounds with no connection.

Unfortunately, it's all very confusing ...

Perhaps it will help to communicate with the cells in the brain from time to time in the near future. That way, I might get a complete picture over time.

I'm just about to end the trance to be taken back to my room when I have an idea.

What if I managed to build up the leg and foot muscles in my body and strengthen them? Then I might be able to walk normally again soon. And because the information transfer of the memories has at least partially worked, building up the muscles in this way could also work.

I use the same technique as I did with the memories, this time concentrating on the leg muscles and ask them to get stronger and grow. First one leg, then the other.

With a feeling of contentment, I think about what else I could do, detached from my body, to speed up the recovery when I realise that I still have a training program to complete in my body today. Because I don't know what time it is, I decide to end the trance so as not to be late.

I am recalling the part of this morning's meditation training that allows me to feel my body again and become aware of space, bringing me back to the physical world, when I feel another set of emotions and feelings, this time very organised and structured. I also sense that these feelings are not coming from my body, but from somewhere else. They are feelings of despair and fear. Someone is feeling these feelings right now! I want to know who it is and I am focusing on their source. As if there were an invisible bond between me and her, I realise after a few seconds that these are Barbara's feelings.

Why is she so afraid? Why is she so desperate? I concentrate myself on Barbara even more and suddenly gain access to an expanded perception. I see my calm meditating body sitting in its place in the room and at the same time, that Barbara lying curled up on the couch at home and crying. It is a quiet weeping interspersed with shorter and longer sobs.

Why is she crying? Is the condition of my body the reason? What can I do to make her feel better?

The only thing I can think of is to send her energy so that she can cope better with the stress of this situation.

I imagine energy flowing away from me and towards her. I imagine how this energy merges with her body. I actually have no idea whether it works like this, but my feeling tells me that she can draw on my energy in this way.

In the first few minutes, her emotional state does not change. Then her sobs slowly decrease until it gradually disappears completely. Now she only cries. I continue to send her energy. After a few minutes, the crying becomes less and finally stops completely. She now lies curled up on the couch and stares into void. Because I am not yet satisfied with her condition, I continue to send her energy. Another few minutes pass. At some point, she sits upright on the couch. Her eyes are red and swollen from crying. After a few minutes, she gets up, goes into the kitchen and prepares something to eat. I'm not really happy with her condition yet, but at least she's well enough now that she can hopefully get on with her everyday life. So I let go of the situation and close myself off to this expanded perception.

That was enough excitement for one meditation session, so I rewind the part of this morning's meditation training that made me feel my body again.

After a few minutes, I feel like I can feel my body normally again and open my eyes. I sit in my seat as I did before the meditation, but I feel weak and tired. Did the meditation take energy? Or was it the energy transfer to Barbara? It doesn't matter! I want to go back to my room and sleep. So I call the nurse.

When we reenter my hospital room, we are surprised by a man sitting on my couch and leafing through one of the magazines. He is wearing trousers that are faded and stained blue. It is also slightly torn in places. He is wearing a white and grey shirt with a strange, also faded inscription on it. The shirt also looks stained. Long, greasy hair falls in his face.

His sitting posture suggests that he won't be leaving this very cosy couch any time soon.

„Well, there he is! The man, the master!", he greets me. Am I an old friend he hasn't seen for years? He gets up from the sofa, comes over to me, bends down to the height of the wheelchair and hugs me, the patches on his armpits right next to my nose.

I intuitively move my upper body slightly to the side to avoid the foul odour.

„What's wrong with you?", he asks me in a loud voice. He leans on the wheelchair with both hands, forcing me to stay in place with him. I find the situation so grotesque that I don't say anything at first and just stare at him. He obviously doesn't like that at all. His expression darkens.

„Is that any way to greet an old friend?" His look becomes even more dark. Suddenly, as if he had just lost his composure for a moment, he smiles at me again:

„Well, we're all old somehow. Or not?"

He laughs out loud and looks at me and the nurse with a grin, which only makes things even more grotesque. I swallow my astonishment and my amazement and answer:

„I was told that I was beaten up."

„Beaten up!", he repeats uncomfortably loud. „Can you remember anything?"

His face darkens again. This time he looks at me angrily and demanding.

„I have the problem that I can't remember anything from my whole life", I reply, this time at almost the same volume as him. „Not even the beatings", I add. He doesn't let up.

„So you don't remember that you were beaten up?" His gaze becomes more and more demanding, as if he's trying to coax the truth out of me with his eyes.

„Yes, that's right! I don't remember anything about being beaten up."

I want to avoid any misunderstanding and therefore formulate the sentence very clearly.

„Well, that is it!", he says in his loud voice, looking very satisfied. He still holds the wheelchair firmly and rocks his upper body up and down slightly, as if he were nodding.

After rocking up and down a few times, he lets go of the wheelchair and clumsily moves past me and the nurse towards the door. As he does so, he looks first at me, then at the nurse with a broad grin and says, again far too loudly:

„I hope they catch the ones who beat you up!"

Then he's gone. The nurse and I look at each other, completely dumbfounded.

„What was that?", she asks me. I answer:

„I have no idea. I hope that wasn't a friend of mine. You'd get scared!"

„That's true!" she agrees. She lifts me back into bed and leaves the room.

Who was this strange man? Judging by his behaviour, he might have something to

84

do with the beating my body. I should find out where he went and whether he actually had anything to do with it. After all, he knows which hospital house room I'm lying in. With this knowledge, he could probably find out more details about me.

Despite being tired and weak, I decide to follow him as a spirit being and maybe find out something that way. I don't want to call the nurse again to take me to the meditation room. I'm sure she has more important things to do than keep driving me somewhere. So I decide to meditate in my room and take the risk of being disturbed. I close my eyes and rewind what I have learnt in order to enter the meditation. It takes a few minutes again until I'm in trance.

Detached from my body, the first thing I do is trying to find the strange man again. I float out of the window of my room and try to find the main entrance to the hospital. Sooner or later he has to leave the building via this entrance.

When I find the entrance, I stay there and wait for him. I am hovering over a large park with wide paths leading to public benches, artistic statues, small children's playgrounds and fountains. The park is surrounded by a wide pavement to which the paths connect. A two-lane road runs parallel to the pavement on one side of the park. Next to the road is another pavement and next to the pavement, directly in front of me, is the main entrance to the hospital. At the level of the park, next to the hospital, there is a bus stop on both sides of the pavement.

Some people are busy walking through the park, others are sitting on the park benches and still others are crossing the road or walking along the pavement. It's a beautiful, sunny day. I, as a spirit being, seem to be invisible, because nobody takes any notice of me.

This is the first time I've seen the hospital from the outside. The main entrance and the front part of the building are surrounded by a glass dome, so you can see some of the activity inside. The rest of the building towards the back looks like the many other brick-built neighbourhood.

I'm surprised that my visitor hasn't turned up at the main entrance yet. Not that he's going to take some side entrance to leave the hospital and I'll miss him.

Just as I'm about to look for side entrances, he comes out through the main entrance. He walks quickly out of the hospital, slows down on the pavement and stops at the bus stop next to people waiting.

He looks briefly at his watch and waits too.

I notice that, unlike my visitor, the others are wearing well-fitting, colour-coordinated clothing and I wonder why his is so different from their.

It takes about ten minutes, then a bus arrives and stops at the bus stop. The doors open and the people waiting, including my visitor, get on. A few seconds later, the bus starts moving again and I follow it.

The journey takes what feels like an eternity. The bus stops again and again at a bus stop to let passengers on and off. Each time it stops, I take extra care to ensure that my visitor doesn't leave the bus too, because I don't want to lose his lane. The bus drives to the city centre. Since the knowledge transfer, I know that there are several opportunities to change to other bus routes there, because my body used to be busy there due to my job. This means I have to pay special attention to my visitor here.

And indeed! He leaves the bus, walks a few metres further and gets further on another bus.

From now on, I follow this bus, which also stops at a bus stop every few minutes at first. The longer the journey takes, the longer the intervals between stops become, which means that the bus covers an increasingly longer distance before letting passengers on and off again.

After a while, the neighbourhood looks increasingly dilapidated and unkempt. Some of the streets and buildings have deep Cracks, people on the pavements are wearing more and more unclean and ill fitting clothes. There is rubbish lying around.

The bus continues to make its way further and further into this area. At some point, when it stops again at a bus stop, my visitor gets off and walks towards a housing estate. His path leads more and more clearly to a dilapidated detached house. When he gets there, he rings the doorbell, which is opened a little later by a man. He talks to him, then he is let in and the door is closed.

I also float through the door into the house and enter a small anteroom that is also threatened by decay. My visitor has already left through a doorless passageway and I float in after him and enter another room.

A large, round table surrounded by chairs is set up in the centre of the room. The table and chairs look to me as if they would normally be in a modern meeting room, while the rest of the room looks as old and dilapidated as the anteroom. My visitor has taken a seat on an old sofa that looks just as worn as the rest of the room. As with the sofa in my hospital room, his sitting position suggests that he feels comfortable on it.

A young man sits on one of the chairs at the large table and takes instructions from an older man, which he types onto a laptop.

The way they are dressed makes them fit perfectly into the image of the modern meeting room.

The man who has just dictated the instructions looks up and addresses my visitor.

„Finally! And? What did you find out?"

Apparently, he is not only the superior of the man in front of the laptop, but also that of my visitor. He straightens up a little so that he is now sitting rather than lying down and answers with amusement:

„The guy has hit the jackpot! He doesn't even know who he is anymore! He's forgotten everything!" His counterpart looks confused.

„What does that mean exactly?"

My visitor, who had just been in a good mood, gets angry.

„Man, he's got amnesia or something!" The supervisor approaches my visitor and turns a chair at the table to take a seat.

„What exactly did he say?"

„No idea! He says he can't remember anything, so it's all good", replies my visitor.

„What do you mean?" the suit guy probes. „What exactly did he say?"

Annoyed by the questions, my visitor drives at him:

„I don't know, man! He doesn't know anything anymore, he said."

The supervisor doesn't put up with his annoyed behaviour and looks at him warningly, whereupon my visitor realises his inappropriate tone.

„Does he only know nothing more about the attack, or does he also know nothing more about his profession? Does he still know how to defend people in court?" asks the superior. My visitor remains silent and shrugs his shoulders ignorantly. There is a short pause while the supervisor considers.

„How is he supposed to get acquittals for our people in future if he has no idea how to do it?", he finally asks.

He gets up from his chair and walks thoughtfully around the room. After a few minutes, he says:

„Damn it! We have to send someone to him again!"

A pause for thought follows. Silence reigns in the room. Their eyes are fixed on the boss. He continues his thoughts:

„But the person must confidently find out what he still know and whether he can still work for us in the future."

Another pause for thought.

„It's best to bring him here. At night. Here we have the advantage that we can easily bribe anyone who notices something despite the darkness."

„Is he to be picked up today?", his assistant interrupts him.

The boss shakes his head after a short pause for thought.

„No! As long as he's in hospital, there are too many potential witnesses. Wait until he's discharged and attack him at his home ... But please! The attack must be well planned. Among other things, you first have to find out what problems we might have to deal with when he's back home."

The boss thinks again.

„This time I will personally lead the attack", he decides. „The fact that there are no witnesses to the first attack, which you idiots performed out in broad daylight, is a stroke of luck. But we won't be that lucky again!"

The boss goes to his assistant and sits next to him on the chair.

„All right, we'll monitor his house from now on. Monitor discreetly! His girlfriend mustn't find out. That way we'll know when he's coming home and can scout the neighbourhood properly. We'll also find out what kind of problems we can expect and can subsequently strike. But guys", he looks at his two colleagues in turn, „wait for my orders! Nobody does anything until I say so! Understood?"

Both nod.

„Good!", He looks satisfied and breaks up the meeting. Everyone leaves the house and goes their separate ways.

I fly back to my body and end the trance.

What kind of meeting was that?

So they're watching my house from now on to find out when I'm coming home! Oh my God!

The nurse comes in and interrupts my thoughts. It's probably time for the next therapy session. I'll have to think about the meeting later. She greets me and lifts me into the wheelchair as usual. I have trouble detaching my thoughts from the meeting and slowly drift into a mild state of shock.

How can I protect myself from another attack? I can't even move reliably! How am I supposed to defend myself in the event of an attack? Or run away?

The nurse takes me to the second floor again. This time it's a different room, much smaller than the rooms I've been in before.

There is a small table in the centre, big enough for two people to sit comfortably opposite each other. On the table are diffe-rent coloured wooden blocks in various sizes and shapes.

Next to it is a pile of large cards with illustrations. On the floor next to the chair on which the therapist is sitting is a grey plastic box with a handle.

The therapist stands up, comes over to me and greets me. It's the same man who is helping me to strengthen my foot and leg muscles. He asks me to take a seat on one of the two chairs and then he sits down on the other while the nurse helps me onto the chair.

„Mr Steiner, you can see some wooden blocks here in front of you."

He runs his open hand over the blocks. „I will now give you various cards. On them you can see building blocks arranged to form a tower.

Please place the building blocks on the table in front of you so that they form the same tower as on the cards. For example, if a building block is shown on its side, please place it in front of you on the same side."

I'm still in some kind of shock and am only marginally aware of what the therapist is saying. He realises this and repeats what he has said. This time I force myself to listen, and when I have understood everything, I nod.

He shows me the first card. It shows five building blocks, one in red, one in blue, one in green and two in yellow. They are stacked in two rows, with the red, blue and green blocks in the bottom row and the two yellow blocks in the top row.

I set up the blocks according to the illustrations in front of me, which I manage to do within a few seconds, although I still notice a certain amount of uncertainty when using my arms and hands. However, they are already easier to move and to coordinate than they were shortly after I woke up from my coma.

The therapist examines my work and nods with satisfaction.

„Very well done."

He makes a note on a pad and hands me the next card. This picture shows eight blocks in the same colours that were used for the last tower, plus two additional blocks in red and one in purple. This time there are four rows on top of each other. The first row again consists of three blocks, again in red, blue and green, placed exactly as on the last card. The second row consists of two blocks in yellow, placed next to each other corner to corner. The two purple blocks rest edge to edge above the second row, reversed to the second row. There is a space about the width of a finger between them.

As I set up the blocks in front of me, I realise that I am having slight difficulties coordinating my arms and hands in the right way. My arms start to tremble slightly just before the end of the finished figure, but I still manage to build it. The therapist takes another close look at the result, nods and writes something down on his pad again.

It goes on like this for a while. At some point, the building blocks turn into upturned plastic cups that have to be built into a tower, or small, long wooden sticks that also have to be stacked in pairs to form a tower.

After each completed task, the therapist nods and makes a note on his pad. I notice more and more, how tired my arm and hand muscles become and that my arms and hands tremble more and more. At the end of the therapy, the trembling is clearly visible and my muscles burn with every movement.

After saying goodbye, the nurse takes me back to my room and lifts me into bed. As I lie in bed, I notice something blocky black on my nightstand with a piece of paper on it. Something is written on it:

Hello, my darling!

Unfortunately, I didn't find you and couldn't wait any longer. Hence the message. The nurses say you can read again!

That's fantastic!

I was actually thinking of bringing a book of short stories to the hospital to read to you, but now you can read for yourself again. Tomorrow I'll bring you some photos and other reading material.
  Maybe that will help you remember again.

I kiss you! I love you!

Your Barbara

I am very happy about her letter. My friend is very special and I'm already looking forward to her visit tomorrow.

Should I tell her about the conversation I overheard? If I do that, I must also tell her about my new abilities as a spirit being.

Should I really do that?

Judging by the conversation between the three unknown men, only I am in danger - so it doesn't affect her. Besides, I don't know how she would react if her boyfriend suddenly had strange powers.

The male nurlse, not the nurse, brings dinner this time. He puts the tray with the dinner on the table as usual, lifts me from the bed, sits me down on one of the chairs, wishes me a bon appetit and leaves the room. There is fish fillet, potatoes and vegetables.

I don't really have appetite, eat a few bites from time to time reluctantly and think about the conversation I overheard between the three unknown men. After a while, I leave half the food, call the nurse and am taken back to bed.

Once in bed, I decide that I won't tell Barbara about it for the time being and will try to get the police to protect me. But how do I do that?

Should I tell the police about the conversation? Doctor Koller has already said that someone wants to talk to me about the attack on me.

If I decide to tell them about the conversation, they will certainly want to know how I was able to eavesdrop on the three strangers when I am barely able to get out of bed, so it is probably better not to mention it. Maybe I can get the police to put me under their protection, when I tell them how I was beaten up. But first I have to find out who did it and why it happened ...

But I'm too tired for that now, I can't think properly. So I decide to get some rest and think about it later again.

I close my eyes and snuggle into the duvet.

When I open my eyes again, I feel rested and more powerful.

Did I sleep and if so, for how long?

I can see through the window that it's dark outside.

Because I am now relatively awake again and feel that I won't be able to fall asleep again straight away, I decide to stimulate the muscle growth in my legs again in a trance and perform the corresponding exercises, which leave me disembodied.

After that, I ask the muscles in my legs to get stronger and grow until I feel like to be tired and able to sleep. I end the trance, close my eyes again and relax.

The next day begins with a sensation.

After the nurse has woken me up, I go to the dining table under his watchful eye and eat my breakfast.

As I walk towards the dining table, I notice that my legs are much easier to move than they were the day before! I can stand and walk!

Admittedly, the whole thing is still a bit wobbly and I have to hold on to something from time to time, but now I no longer absolutely need the nurse to move me around. I can also move my arms and hands quite well and safely, and they feel more powerful than before.

With this motivation, I head straight to the bathroom to brush my teeth and take a shower. On the way there, I pause every now and then when I realise that my legs are getting too weak and hold on to the handrails on the wall.

When I get to the bathroom, I brush my teeth and take a shower sitting up, then I go back to my bed.

I also want to change my clothes, but first my legs, arms and hands need a bit of a rest. Because the nurse has left the room at some point, I decide to change a little later.

I continue the previous day's thoughts about getting help from the police and come to the conclusion that I will call them at the next opportunity. That's all I can do at the moment.

The last few days have been very exciting, so I close my eyes and relax a little ...

After about thirty minutes there is a knock at the door, but unlike the previous visitors, the knocker is waiting outside.

„Yes, come in!", I call out.

The door opens and two policemen enter the room and come to my bed.

„Good morning. Are you Mr Wilhelm Steiner?"

I answer with a curt „yes".

„Hello, Mr Steiner," the policeman greets me again and shakes my hand. „Police, third district, Balduinstrasse. I'm Chief Inspector Rudolf Mayer, and this is my colleague Hendrik Bauer. We'd like to ask you a few questions about the incident before your coma."

The gentlemen probably don't realise yet that I would like to have answers to these questions myself, I think, and explain my memory problem to them.

„But ... ", I continue, „the fact that I was beaten up like that could also mean that I'm still in danger. Is there any way the police can protect me?", I put my plan into action now, not on the phone.

A short pause follows, during which the policeman thinks. He writes something on

103

a small pad he has brought with him and says:

„We will look into the possibility of police protection for you. But as long as you can't give us any details, it looks rather bad, because we have no clues as to whether your lives could actually be in danger", he explains to me. „Until we have proof that organised crime is behind it, police protection is often not possible. But if you think of anything else, no matter what, please call this number."

He hands me a business card, then they both say goodbye and leave the room.

The policeman's words make me think: if I could reconstruct exactly what happened during that attack, I might get the police protection I've been longing for. Perhaps the cells in my brain can now be persuaded to release this information. At least that's what I have to try. A glance at the therapy schedule tells me that I only have a short time left until the next session, so I give my cells some time to rest until after the therapy. My idea is that after a mental rest, they will perhaps be more capable of releasing information. So I try to relax and calm down.

When it's time for therapy, the nurse comes to pick me up. I'm already dressed and sitting on a chair waiting for him.

He is obviously very impressed by my healing successes, because he greets me with the words:

„So, Mr Steiner, you're giving the word healing a whole new meaning!"

He drives the wheelchair to me.

„But please still sit in the wheelchair when I take you to therapy now. The therapist has to assess you first and then decide whether you can walk on your own in future."

Although it annoys me that I still have to use this aid, I sit down in the chair and let myself be driven to the second floor.

Once there, the therapist greets me again.

„Hello, Mr Steiner! You look well! How are you doing?"

„Very good!" I say euphorically and proudly tell him about my successes.

„Okay, that sounds very good! Let me see what you can do. Please take a step or two."

I prepare to stand up. The nurse and the therapist want to support me and give me a hand, but I wave them off.

„I can do it on my own now", I say, whereupon they both let go of my arms.

„But be careful, Mr Steiner!", the therapist advises me. „Don't fall down despite your confidence!"

Their posture suggests that they are ready to catch me at any time should I fall.

I shift my weight onto my legs, support myself with my arms on the armrests of the wheelchair and stand up. It's a bit harder than getting up from the bed or the chair in my room after eating, as you sit very low in a wheelchair. Nevertheless, I manage it, albeit shakily.

The therapist observes what is happening and signals to the nurse to support me. Then he opens one of the two doors and disappears behind it.

A few minutes later, he comes back with a rolling device. In the meantime, I have sat back down in the wheelchair with the nurse's help, as standing is still tiring and the wheelchair seat is too low for me to sit down on my own.

The therapist places the rolling device in front of me, looks at me, then back at the device and then adjusts the handles that are attached to it.

„There you go, Mr Steiner! This is a rollator. Please hold on to these handles as you walk", he says, touching the handles of the device. „This should stabilise your stance. Please try walking up and down the hall with the rollator on your own."

I don't need to be told twice. Anything that helps me to become more independent is most welcome. So I push myself up onto my feet again, hold on to the rollator and actually have a firm footing. Full of anticipation at finally being able to walk without the nurse's help, I now take a few steps with the rollator. I manage quite well.

The therapist and the nurse walks close to me, always ready to catch me if I should fall. After a few metres, the therapist disappears again while the nurse continues to keep an eye on me and returns shortly afterwards with an chair, which he places in place of the wheelchair.

„If it gets too strenuous, please sit down on the chair, rest and start again", he explains to me.

He banishes the wheelchair to a corner of the room.

I walk back and forth on my own for quite a while until it gets too tiring. Then I sit down on the chair, rest and start my walk allover again. The therapist and the nurse walk alongside me at first, but soon keep their distance and then just watch me walk.

When saying goodbye, the therapist says:

„Mr Steiner, congratulations on your progress! Unbelievable! It's best to take the rollator to your room and exercise whenever you like. But please pay attention to enough rest breaks! If you can't take any more, just sit down for a moment and rest ... And please stay away from walking outside in the open air."

He shakes my hand.

„Otherwise, I'll see you at the next therapy session. Good luck until then and goodbye."

The nurse takes me back to my room in my wheelchair.

As good as the therapy went, I'm still a bit annoyed that my legs are still not strong enough and I can't walk on my own.

Once in the room and after the nurse has left, I do what I had planned to do before the therapy. I want to stimulate my brain cells to reveal information about the incident, as the police officers called it.

So I go into trance again. Once I am in this state, I concentrate on the cells in my brain and instruct them to disclose the memories of the incident. It takes a few minutes, but I actually get some information. There are pictures and sounds, and this time they come in a more organised way than last time:

I see some attackers, unfortunately very indistinctly. The visible memories are rotated as if the body is already lying on the ground and seeing everything from the side. Clothing and other features of the attackers are unrecognisable. Even now, lying on the ground, the figures do not stop kicking the body. That much is clear recognizable from the memory. After a few kicks, the memory comes to an end.

Other parts of the memory, such as voices, are too unclear to be analysed properly.

Unfortunately, it's not a particularly big gain. I had hoped for more. Much more!

The only thing that seems certain is that there were several attackers. I think about what else I could do to get information about the attack, but I feel like I can't think properly. Because I want to move around and I am not allowed to go outside yet, I decide to walk up and down in the room with the rollator. After a few rounds, I rest on a chair and then start over again. This is how I spend the rest of the time until lunch.

The nurse who brings me my food tells me that I am also allowed to walk back and forth in the corridor outside my room, which I do after eating. The nurse places a chair in front of my room where I can rest from time to time.

After a while, having lost track of time, I see Barbara coming towards me with open arms and an incredibly happy smile. As I get closer, I notice her great figure and pretty face again.

She takes me in her arms, gives me a kiss on the lips and says happily:

„You can walk already! I'm so proud of you and your progress. I love you!"

I am very happy that she is visiting me and realise that I have missed her. I would love to tell her about what I have experienced in the last few days. About the trip as a ghost and the fact that I overheard the criminals.

Again, I decide not to tell her because the fear of how she might react when she realises she has a friend with strange powers is still too big.

We go into my room together. She sits down on the couch next to my bed. At first I tend to lie down on the bed, but I've done that too often recently, so I decide in favour of the couch after all. So I sit down next to Barbara. I give her a kiss on the lips and say:

„I'm really happy that you're here! I've missed you."

Her smile widens and her eyes begin to sparkle. She sits down very close to me, puts her head on my shoulder and says:

„I'm glad you're feeling so well again."

„I'm very happy about that too", I say. „And thank you for visiting me every day, by the way. I like that, it makes me feel less alone!"

„That goes without saying, my darling. I love you!", she replies.

We hug each other. Her embrace is so good for me that I close my eyes and concentrate on it, savouring it. We linger in each other's arms for a while until I suddenly feel something soft and warm on my lips and open my eyes. Barbara has opened her mouth slightly and is playing tenderly with my lips. I open my mouth too, whereupon my eyes close again and my tongue starts to play with hers. Strong feelings of love and security awaken in me and I let myself be carried away.

After this great experience, we sit closely together on the couch for a while and she tells me about our holidays, about how she was present in court a few times as a spectator and watched me work as a lawyer. She also talks about how I introduced her to my parents and she introduced me to hers. She also tells me that my parents live about 500 kilometres away from here and that they only visited once while I was still in a coma. She tells me about my friends and how I introduced them to her. My friends had also visited here during my coma.

At some point she remembers that she has brought a photo album with her. We look at it together. She tells me the story behind each picture. We both hope that this might bring back a few memories. Maybe even a few more.

The stories and looking at the photos make me tired. So after a while I go back to bed.

She sits down next to me on a chair and holds my hand for a long time. When she has to leave, we kiss goodbye and tell each other how much we've enjoyed our time together today.

I think about the photos she showed me for a long time that afternoon. About how little I know about our life together. I'm thinking about how dependent people are on the passage of time when a thought occurs to me:

What if I were to run back time myself to find out exactly what happened? To find out who did so much to my body that I ended up in hospital. I could then explain it to the police in detail and maybe get the police protection I was hoping for. I have no idea if I'm capable of manipulating time, but it's the only thing I can think of, so I want to at least try.

When I am travelling in space as a spirit being, for example from the hospital room out through the window and hovering over the park, it works by thinking that I want to do exactly that, and then it happens. What if I were to try the exact same thing in relation to time?

I'll just try it out now. First with something simple. Maybe just a few minutes travelling back in time, or maybe until I reach the time when Barbara said goodbye to me today.

I go into trance again. Once I've done that, I imagine the situation when my girlfriend was still in the room talking to me, just before we said goodbye. I want time to change at this exact moment. I wait a while and watch to see if anything happens. Nothing happens. Either I can't travel in time or I'm doing something wrong.

I'm thinking about it ... Building up my muscles has, in addition to the thoughts about it, also meant communicating with the cells of the muscles are needed. Perhaps this is also necessary when travelling through time.

So once again. I visualise the situation in question and send out a request in my mind for the time to change at this point. As I do this, I observe what happens.

Nothing happens for the first few seconds. I'm about to give up when suddenly my body moves without me doing anything. It makes exactly the same movements that I made a few minutes ago, before my trance - only backwards! I look at my watch. The minute hand of the clock is also moving very slowly backwards. So time is actually going backwards! I watch this for a while longer because I want to make sure that the time really has been turned back by the time I say goodbye to my girlfriend.

Suddenly the door opens and Barbara comes into the room walking backwards. She has her upper body slightly bent forwards, as if she were actually walking forwards. When she reaches my body by the bed, his hand is sucked into hers. Now the action stops.

Barbara holds the hand of my body in hers and has her lips slightly open as if she is about to say something. The minute hand on the clock also stands still. That was exactly the moment I had in mind as the point at which time was to be turned back. So it worked!

Now I would like to know whether it also works to let time run forwards again. Again, I mentally imagine the situation in which I wanted to let time run backwards and ask time to change at this point.

And indeed, something happens again. My girlfriend and the minute hand start to move again, this time forwards. Barbara lets go of my body's hand and walks towards the door. My body makes a few more movements until it reaches the right time and then stops again. So the test was successful in both directions.

Now back to when my body was beaten up. So now I imagine the time just before my body was beaten up and ask time to change again.

Again, I watch my body and the minute hand move. The hand and my body moves slowly backwards in time.

However, I notice that the speed at which time moves backwards is the same speed at which it normally moves forwards. Because I want to travel back to a more distant point in time, I need to go backwards a little faster. So I concentrate on increasing the speed and ask time again to fulfil my wish. After a few moments, the scenery does indeed move noticeably faster. I do this a few more times until the travelling speed is fast enough.

My body keeps leaving the room backwards and then coming back in, and Barbara does the same. At some point, the plasters are applied to the face and the rest of the body and briefly then exchanged for bandages. Soon my face is almost completely covered and the medical equipment is connected to my body. Doctors come in and out of the room.

The body and bed are moved out of the room and back in again for examinations. Visitors come and go. At some point, the body is moved out of the room and never returned.

A few seconds pass before I realise that this must be the day the body was brought in. So the day of the beating! That means I have to stay with my body and not lose it!

So I float through the closed room door into the corridor. To my horror, I can't see the body anywhere. Have I waited too long?

I must try to find him again!

After a few minutes of unsuccessful searching, I decide to go to the main entrance of the hospital. After all, the body has to appear there at some point. So I float back to my room and through the window until to the main entrance. I am now above the park. The people there are also doing their work backwards. Those who are on their way somewhere are walking backwards with their bodies leaning slightly forwards. An old woman sits on a park bench and feeds pigeons with pieces of stale bread. This also happens backwards: the pigeons do not pick up the pieces of bread to eat them, but lay them on the ground and stumble on backwards. Other visitors walk their dogs backwards. The cars and motorbikes on the road also drive backwards.

While the time continues to roll back and I wait for my body, an ambulance reverses out of the back of the hospital with its blue lights flashing and continues on its way towards the city centre. But I don't see my body anywhere! It should have arrived at the main entrance by now.

Because I can't think of anything better to do, I search the hospital for side entrances.

Earlier I saw an ambulance driving away, which means that there must be at least one emergency entrance for vehicles.

At the same time as this thought, I suddenly realise that my body has probably left the hospital in the ambulance that left earlier. So I decide to follow the ambulance.

But it's already out of earshot. I remember that I noticed earlier that the car was heading towards the city centre. So I now head in that direction at high speed.

To find him faster, I pause the time travel. When I reach the car, I let it run backwards again and follow it.

At some point, the car stops in a large square. Lots of people are busily going their separate ways, backwards of course. Two paramedics and a doctor get out of the back of the ambulance and unload my body. He is lying on a stretcher and looks terrible, his clothes and face are covered in blood and his face is very swollen.

The paramedics roll the stretcher and body backwards across the large square into a side alley. Passers-by walking backwards acknowledge the action with a quick glance and then continue on their way. Once in an alley, the paramedics lower the stretcher to ground level and lift the body onto the tarmac. The doctor kneels down to him and apparently checks his injuries. After a few seconds, he stands up again, the doctor and paramedics walk backwards to the car and drive away, also backwards, with blue lights flashing.

I stay on site. I want to know who did this to the body and why. To do this, I have to wait until time has been turned back far enough for the perpetrators to return to the body.

No-one appears for a few seconds and the hustle and bustle in the large square continues merrily backwards. Then a figure comes walking backwards, the back of his head covered with a hood and a triangular scarf covering his neck, nose and mouth.

The cut of his clothes, his movements and his gait indicate hat it could be a man.

He takes a device out of his jacket pocket and presses something on it. Then he puts it to his ear, pushes the covering over his mouth to one side and speaks, so the device is apparently a telephone. I can't understand what he's saying because he's talking backwards. After a series of sentences, he presses a few buttons on the phone and puts it back in his pocket. Meanwhile, two more hooded figures, apparently also men, come walking backwards. He says something to them, also backwards of course. Then one of them starts kicking the body. The other two join in after a few seconds. All three hit the chest, stomach and face with their feet. You can see from the face that time is running backwards because the injuries are getting less. After some kicks and punches, my body is now upright again and no longer injured, one of the figures hugs him with one arm and shouts emphatically led backwards out of the alley. The body has raised its shoulders as if unconsciously trying to protect itself from the masked man's embrace. The hooded man says something to him that I unfortunately can't understand either. Now everyone else moves backwards out of the alley. The man leading my body out of the alley gesticulates and continues to talk to him. When he reaches the centre of the large square, he lets go of the body and all three hooded men move away. They push their hoods back and push their collars down so that their faces are visible. Surprised, I recognise the face of the man who visited me in hospital. I had already assumed that he must have something to do with my body's coma. Here is the confirmation! All three of them are walking backwards in the opposite direction to the body with increasing speed.

Here I now have to change the time flow and let time run forwards again, because here I will presumably find out why the whole thing is happening and who these guys are. So I let time move forward again at normal speed and watch what happens.

The three figures cover themselves up again and quickly return to the body, now walking forwards in their usual manner. One of the figures raises his arm and embraces him. My body reacts with surprise and amazement. He asks:

„What...?" He looks round and sees the two other figures. „You represented Moe in court, didn't you?", asks the figure hugging him.

My body is confused: „What, in court? Could be ... Who is Moe?"

„Mohamed Shenko! You represented him in court ... didn't you?", asks the hugger again.

„Mohamed Shenko?" the body asks, still visibly confused and surprised. But slowly he realises who is meant.

„Oh yes! I represented him. For drug dealing, if I remember correctly."

As he talks, he tries to free himself from the embrace. But the hugger persists. He pushes him towards the alley while talking, from which they had previously emerged when time was running backwards.

„Why do you want to know?" my body asks.

The hugger doesn't answer and instead says reproachfully:

„Well, you messed up! He was found guilty!"

„The evidence was overwhelming. There was nothing more I could do", defends the body, which has now arrived at the entrance to the small alleyway accompanied by the three figures. The hugger gets angry and pushes the body into the alley.

„Your job was to get him released. You didn't manage that, and now you have to pay for that!"

He slams his clenched fist into the stomach of the body, which screams in pain and falls to the ground, hunched over. He remains huddled there, whimpering. The attackers follow up. One of them beats the body with his fists and as soon as my body leaves the protective crouched position to protect his face from the attacks, another follows up with kicks to the abdomen and chest and other parts of the body.

All three work on their victim again and again in this way. At some point I don't hear any more screams or whimpers from the body, it's probably unconscious by now.

„Ok, guys, stop!" suddenly says the previously hugging one. „We don't want to kill him. We just want him to realise that he'll have to do a better job next time."

The attackers let go of the body.

„All right, let's go to the getaway car now! And get rid of your clothes as we discussed!", he instructs his colleagues.

The two leave the alley. He stays behind, takes his phone out of his jacket pocket, dials a number and waits for the other person to pick up.

„Hello, I've just walked past Bertholdgasse 4, someone is lying on the floor covered in blood", he finally says in an impassive voice and adds a few seconds later:

„Unfortunately, I can't tell you any more. I'm late", he presses a button and lets the phone disappear back into his pocket while he lets the mask fall over his mouth. Then he also leaves the alley.

Now I've learnt what I wanted to know and I'm rewinding time to the present.

Once there, my body is back in bed, just as it was at the beginning of the journey, and I end the trance.

Back in my body, I pick up the policeman's business card and the phone from the box next to my bed, dial the number and wait for it to be answered.

„Chief Inspector Rudolf Mayer", a voice announces.

„Greetings! This is Wilhelm Steiner. It's about the attack on me. You wanted me to call you if I remember anything again."

A brief silence at the other end of the line, then the inspector probably remembers who I am.

„Ah, yes! Hello, Mr Steiner!", he greets me. „Just a moment, please!"

He audibly rummages through something and finally says:

„All right, thanks for waiting. We're ready to go. Please tell me what you remember."

I describe the experience to him as if it came from my memory. I leave out all the information about the time travel. I want him to believe me and not hang up on me straight away. He has a few questions in between and after my story, which I try to answer. At some point he has everything he needs ... As far as the police protection is concerned, he tells me that the documents need to be checked and that will take at least a few hours, but if the decision is negative, it could take a few days. My signature is also required, which is why he will come to the hospital tomorrow morning. He then says goodbye and hangs up.

Now that the police have all the information and can at least write the report, I'm a bit calmer. Nevertheless, there's a good chance that I won't get police protection, which I need to be prepared for when I'm discharged from hospital at the latest. Being able to move normally again would be a good start, but not enough preparation for my situation. I need to be able to prevent someone from physically attacking me.

My plan is to spend one half of the day training physically and the other half training my mental abilities. If I manage to travel through time, then I must also be able to protect myself from attacks.

By the time I am discharged from hospital at the latest, I would like to be fully physically recovered and have a decent level of mental capacity so that I can arm myself against such attacks in the future.

It is now afternoon. The hands on the clock are at 04:30. I look at the therapy schedule and realise that no therapy is scheduled for today. That explains, why no nurse has picked me up yet.

Because I want to move around and not spend all my time in bed, I decide to spend the rest of the day walking up and down the room and the corridor to exercise my legs. When I need a break, I read the short stories for a while and then continue my workout.

During one of the visits to the corridor, a nurse gives me a document with an appointment for me to see Dr Koller the next day at nine o'clock in the morning.

As I read the lines, I fold the note in half and place it on the chair in front of my room.

I am surprised! What could Doctor Koller want to discuss with me? He usually comes straight to my bedside when there's something to talk about. He has probably changed the treatment plan because of my great progress and would now like to discuss the new plan with me. That will be it.

I spend the rest of the day following my plan and walking up and down the corridor, with breaks when it gets too tiring and when there's food, of course.

Chapter 3:

Dismissal

The next day begins as usual with morning hygiene and breakfast. Then it's time for mental strength training. But before I go into trance, I think about which powers I could use to defend myself. Which powers would help me to ensure my physical integrity after my release?

It would be good to have something like a shield to defend myself and some way to attack back ... First I'll take care of the shield:

I put myself into trance.

Now it's time to experiment. How could such a shield work?

Thinking logically, I could succeed by thickening the air in a certain area so that it is harder to penetrate than usual. That wouldn't stop the attackers, but it would at least hinder them and I could use the time this gave me to escape.

So I try it and concentrate on a hand-sized area directly in front of my body at chest height and try to analyse the air there in meaningfully small units. Once I have succeeded, I want to duplicate these units.

Again, it's as if I know what it takes. Similar to the energy transfer from me to Barbara a few days ago, I use my energy to multiply these small air units for a few minutes.

To test the result, I have to use any part of my body. My hand seems to be the most suitable, so I try to move it, but it doesn't move because I'm in a trance and therefore detached from my body. Ending the trance to test it and then putting myself back into trance seems too much effort, so I try to release only one part of my body from the trance, namely my arm and my hand.

I use the same technique that would otherwise bring me completely out of trance. But this time only in relation to the arm and hand.

It's a strange feeling to only feel one hand and one arm - as if my body only consisted of them.

But now back to the protective shield. I press my hand on the area where the protective shield should be and indeed ... My hand noticeably pushes something away, but the resistance is far too easy to penetrate. So I continue duplicating for a few more minutes and test the result again.

The resistance of the shield is now greater than before, but still not great enough.

After a few more attempts, I'm relatively satisfied for today. I do need quite a bit of muscle power to overcome the air barrier, which should at least buy me some time in a serious case.

Next, I want to acquire a skill that can be used as an attack. The first thing that comes to mind is to make objects fly through the air and turn them into projectiles.

Unfortunately, I have no idea how this could be realised at the moment, so I end the trance, but take to try again later. So instead of practising the attack now, I start with the physical training. To do this, I walk up and down the corridor outside my room again.

At some point I am too tired to move and lie down in bed to rest until the male nurse wakes me up. He has a wheelchair with him.

„I know you don't necessarily need the wheelchair, Mr Steiner, but please sit down anyway so that we can make faster progress, because the doctor doesn't like to wait. He has a lot to do", he says, emphasising his words with a wave of his hand. I do him a favour and let him drive me to my appointment.

When we arrive at the doctor's room, the nurse knocks on the door. Doctor Koller opens shortly afterwards and invites me in.

„Good morning, Mr Steiner. I've already heard about your amazing progress! Please come in."

He points with his open hand to an empty space in front of his desk. The nurse takes me there and leaves the room. The doctor takes a seat in his chair behind the desk.

„Mr Steiner, how are you?", he begins the conversation.

„I'm doing quite well with my walking and my hands, thank you! And it's getting better every day", I report proudly.

„How are your memories?", asks the doctor.

„Unfortunately, I'm still in a very bad way ...", I reply, „I remember some things, but I still can't remember my life."

„Please don't stress about this, because it delays the process. What can help are pictures, photos or sounds that are familiar to you from the past. But once again! Don't stress about it. The calmer you are, the better you will be able to remember", he says.

After a short pause, during which he operates the computer on his desk, he continues:

„Mr Steiner, I think it would be good for your further recovery if you were in familiar environment. The sounds, smells, the surroundings themselves, people you know, all these things can bring back memories. I would therefore like to release you tomorrow or the day after. You would take home the walking aid that you already use and a call aid. This is a device that is attached to your wrist like a watch and has a push button.

When you press the button, it alerts the emergency services, who then come to your home and help you if you fall or something similar happens, for example. As far as I know, you also have your girlfriend at home who can support you."

It surprises and shocks me that he wants to release me already. Not because I don't think I'm physically ready yet, but because I need a few more days to improve my mental capacity.

I have to somehow persuade the doctor to keep me in hospital for another day or two without telling him about my condition. My special skills.

„You want to release me? Already now? It's not even a week since I woke up from my coma. Isn't that too soon?"

„I don't think so. You can always use the call device anyway if you have any problems at home", is his short answer.

„How much longer can I stay here?", I want to know.

„Well, I'll write the doctor's letter today. You have to sign out at the administration office tomorrow at the latest, and then you'll be officially released from the hospital", he explains.

I sit there pensively and remain silent.

„Do you have any questions?"

Completely absorbed in myself, I shake my head.

„Very good! ... Mr Steiner, good luck with your recovery and all the best!"

He shakes my hand and calls the nurse, who takes me and the wheelchair back to my room. Once there, I go back to bed. I'm frustrated, because of the shock.

The thought of being sacked tomorrow runs deep. As soon as Barbara visits me today, I'll tell her the news. But for now I want to go to bed and digest the shock.

Lying in bed, I keep tossing and turning from one side to the other. My thoughts can't rest because I keep thinking about the conversation I overheard and about being released tomorrow.

I reassure myself by promising myself to build up my protective shield as quickly and as strongly as possible.

After a while, there's a knock on the door and Barbara comes in. She smiles broadly when she sees me, comes to the bed and kisses me.

„Hello, darling!"

I greet her too and give her a hug. I'm very pleased that she's here, now I can tell her about my imminent release.

„How are you?" she asks me.

„Well, I'am fine" I reply. „I will be released tomorrow. I heard that earlier, but I'm not ready yet. I'd like to stay here for a few more days."

She pulls up a chair and sits down next to my bed.

„Why are you being released after such a short time? You only woke up from your coma a few days ago?"

„I told the doctor that too! But he's of the opinion that I've recovered sufficiently and my memories will probably come back faster at home than here in hospital", I explain to her.

She takes my hand and thinks about my words.

„It still seems premature to me", she finally says.

„At least the doctor doesn't leave me completely helpless. I get the walking aid that I already use here to take home with me, as well as a call aid."

„A call aid?", she asks, „What's that?"

„The doctor said it was a push button that was attached to my wrist like a watch and that if I fell, for example, I could use it to alert the emergency services, who would then help me on site."

„At least something", she says, „but if you have to go home tomorrow, that also means you'll need help at home. Should I take a few days off?"

„I don't think that's necessary. Physically, I'm definitely well enough to manage on my own ...", I falter in mid-sentence.

Even though I really want to tell her about my abilities and my impending abduction, I'm still afraid of her reaction, and if I go on talking now, I'll have to tell her about it. She will then surely want to know what makes me think that I am threatened with violence again, whereupon I will have to tell her about my abilities as a spirit being ... But do I really want that?

Her eyes change, she probably expects me to keep talking, so all I can do now is tell her about it ...

„But I'm not safe from further attacks at home. The people who beat me into a coma back then are planning to kidnap me!"

She looks at me in disbelief.

„How do you know that? The police don't even know who exactly did it."

„Because I had the opportunity to eavesdrop on the criminals when they were busy planning this new attack on me", I explain to her.

She continues to look at me in disbelief.

„You were able to eavesdrop on them? Here in the hospital? And how do you know that they were the ones who attacked you?"

I tell Barbara everything from the beginning. About how I first discovered and used my abilities in trance to heal my leg muscles, how I followed my visitor as a spirit being and overheard the conversation, and how I am now in the process of acquiring protective mental abilities and those that I can use as a weapon.

When I've finished my story, I look at her face and assume I can see complete disbelief.

„Wait a minute! Wait a minute!" She raises her hands defensively and stares at me questioningly ... As if she hadn't found the answer in my face, she finally asks:

„Is this a joke? Don't make such nonsense with me! It's not funny!"

„No, it's not a joke!", I say emphatically, whereupon she crosses her arms in front of her chest.

„So you're trying to convince me that you can leave your body? You can heal yourself?", she asks angrily.

Apparently she doesn't believe me.

„Prove it to me!", she says suddenly.

„Prove to me that you really have these abilities!"

But how am I supposed to prove that to her?

Perhaps by creating a protective shield directly in front of her. When she realises that there is a resistance in the air in front of her, she will surely be convinced.

I tell her that I need to calm down now and put myself into a trance.

It took a while, but when finished, I manifest a body sized protective shield directly in front of her, release the lower part of my head from the trance so that I can talk to her and say, that she can try now:

„I have created a protective shield in front of you. You should feel a resistance there."

Barbara obviously didn't expect me to speak to her now, because she flinches.

She then bends forward a little so that she can feel the area in front of her. I recognise from her facial expression that she didn't expect to actually feel something in front of her. She waves a hand in front of her, whereupon her hand is obviously braked by the shield. Barbara's eyes widen and she moves closer to the shield.

„What the ...", she doesn't finish the sentence. Her eyes move alternately to me and back to the shield a few times to test the resistance again.

„How... how do you do that?"

Because it would be far too long to explain that to her now, I'll just say:

„I'll tell you about it tomorrow at home. Until then, I'll try to train as much as possible and work on my mental skills."

She nods sympathetically.

„That makes sense, of course! Is there anything I can do at home to make you safer?"

I think about it for a few seconds, then shake my head:

„I don't think so. At least I can't think of anything at the moment."

„Then I'll at least change the alarm system code. Maybe that will help."

I have no idea what she means by alarm system, but I nod anyway. Because I know the word alarm, I can imagine what she is trying to tell me.

As Barbara prepares to leave, she asks:

„When am I supposed to pick you up tomorrow?"

After a moment's thought, I reply:

„I want to sleep longer this time and will sign out afterwards. I'll have lunch at the hospital and then I'll be ready."

„All right, then I'll pick you up around one o'clock in the afternoon."

I agree and nod.

Just before she leaves the door, she asks:

„Shall I bring you something to wear from home? For the journey home?"

Again I think for a moment.

„Yes, please. Just a pair of halfway usable trousers and something for my upper body. You'll find something, I think."

„Really? Something? You're usually so vain!"

Another word I don't understand.

Vain. I decide not to ask her what the word means, but just say:

„Right now, I just want to go home and be safe there ..."

After Barbara has left, I want to rest a bit and read the short stories again. Sometime before lunch, the policeman comes to get my signature, as agreed the day before.

I spend the afternoon and evening training my muscles, improving my protective shield and resting in between.

Unfortunately, as the shield improves, it turns out that the idea of placing the air units closer and closer together to make the wall more stable has its limits.

So I really need a new idea here!

I go to bed early that evening. I want to finally leave the hospital and work with Barbara on securing our house and perhaps also on my mental abilities together, as she might have ideas that I can't think of at the moment.

After a very restless night, in which I often wake up and roll from side to side in bed, it slowly gets light outside. I try to sleep until the nurse brings me breakfast, eat it, get dressed, take a shower and make my way to the hospital administration to checkout.

On the way there, I realise that my legs are working very well again. In my opinion, they are strong enough that I should be able to walk without a walking device, but I'm not going to try that in hospital.

If I can actually walk without help, it's early enough to try it at home. Otherwise I might not be able to take the rollator home with me, and that's too unsafe for me. I leave the room and look for the signs in the corridor to find the right way to the administration.

I see the signs on the wall of the corridor, a few metres to the left of the entrance door to my room. It lists all the hospital departments in a two-column list in black lettering on a coloured background, with each department having its own colour.

I look for the lettering for „Administration". This is written on a green background. So I follow the corresponding floor markings that lead me to the elevator, which I have often used together with the nurse, and enter it with my rollator. Inside, I notice coloured markings next to the floor selection buttons for the first time. I had obviously completely missed them before. I choose the floor with the green marking and drive to the ground floor.

As I leave the lift, I see a long corridor in front of me with lots of doors to the left and right with signs on them. The green floor markings for „Administration" lead to the end of the corridor and through a passageway, so I follow the markings.

Next I come to a large, multi-storey hall. The walls are several storeys high and converge to forma glass dome roof over the entire area. These are probably the glass outer walls of the hospital, which I have already seen as ghost.

I turn round and see a row of floors. Each floor in this building apparently ends here at a stone railing. The different floors are connected by a staircase that leads to the ground floor and ends a few metres from the entrance to the hospital.

An information area can be seen on good distance from the entrance, which consists of a round table with three workstations in the centre. One of them is occupied by an employee. He is typing something into a computer with concentration.

Judging by the markings on the walls, I am now in the administrative area of the hospital and I am looking for a door labelled

„Checkout" because I assume I have to checkout there. To do this, I walk close enough to the doors with my rollator to be able to read the signs. At some point, the employee at the information desk notices this, so he looks in my direction and asks me:

„Is there anything I can do for you?"

I turn to him.

„I'm looking for the checkout station."

„It's there", he points to a door at the other end of the hall.

With a „Thank you!", I make my way there with my rollator. When I reach the right door, I knock and enter. It's a long room with a few desks lined up along its length. In front of and behind them are a chair and a computer and a printer on each of the desks. A lady is sitting at one of the desks, the others are unoccupied. I push the rollator there and sit down on the chair.

The employee smiles at me and asks:

„What can I do for you?"

„I'd like to checkout", I reply.

„All right. What's your name?"

„Wilhelm Steiner."

She says „Thank you" and types something into the computer.

„Okay, good! The doctor's letter is already in the system. When would you like to checkout?"

„Today at one o'clock in the afternoon." She types something into the computer again.

„It says here that you can take the rollator you already use and a call aid home with you."

She looks at me and explains:

„The call assistance works as follows: As soon as you are at home, please call this number."

She gives me a piece of paper with a telephone number.

„You can use it to contact the company that will install and set up the emergency call system for you."

I nod and say:

„Okay, all right."

The employee turns back to the computer.

After a few entries, the printer starts. When it's finished, she takes the page and hands it to me with the words:

„This is confirmation that you have accepted the rollator and the call aid. Please sign here, I'll get the call aid in the meantime."

She points with a pen in hand to a place on the printout where my name is written. I sign my name as requested, while she goes to fetch the call aid from an adjoining room.

When she returns, she is carrying a box in both hands. She hands it to me, sits down at her desk, takes the signed note and types something into the computer again. I think about how I can put the box in my room and decide to put them in the basket of my roller door.

After a few entries, the employee turns to me again:

„Do you have any questions?"

I think about it for a moment, but I can't think of any.

„No, not for now."

She uses the computer again, whereupon the printer on her desk ejects another page, which she hands to me and says:

„This is your checkout certificate. You can submit this to your insurance company."

I take the paper and put it in the basket of my rollator alongside with the emergency call device. Then I say goodbye to her and make my way back to my room.

Once there, I still have time until lunch.

I decide to get some more rest until then. Muscle training or training on my protective shield is useless at the moment because Barbara arrives here soon, and I want to be rested by then so that I can continue working on both again when I am at home.

After a while, the nurse brings lunch. It's just before one o'clock. I enjoy it and then wait - reading the short stories - for Barbara to pick me up.

And then the time has come! There's a knock on the door and Barbara comes into the room with sparkling eyes. She smiles more broadly than I've ever seen before.

She's obviously delighted that I'm coming home. She has a suitcase with her, which she puts on the bed after we say hello. Than she says:

„In there is the clothing you told me to bring to change."

I open the suitcase, take out a pair of blue trousers, socks, something for my upper body and shoes and put everything on.

Meanwhile, Barbara packs up my belongings and when we've finished, we leave the room together, me at the rollator, and go to the elevator to go the ground floor.

Once there, we walk through the long corridor, past the information area, out of the hospital and outside.

The sun is shining. It's a beautiful, warm afternoon. Something is blinding my eyes, so I close them. My skin feels warm. It must be the sun. It's a lovely feeling! I stop and enjoy the warmth and smile. After a while, I feel Barbara's hand on mine.

„I'm glad you're starting to enjoy your life again", she says. „Come on, let's go home!"

Will
continued in episode 2 ...